Merlin

This series is for my riding friend
Shelley, who cares about all animals.

ISBN-13: 978-0-545-07931-0
ISBN-10: 0-545-07931-4

All rights reserved. Published by Scholastic Inc.,
557 Broadway, New York, NY 10012.
SCHOLASTIC and associated logos are trademarks and/or registered trademarks
of Scholastic Inc. Lexile is a registered trademark of MetaMetrics, Inc.

12 11 10 9 8 7 6 5 4   12 13 14/0

Printed in the U.S.A.
First Scholastic printing, March 2009

Merlin

Tina Nolan
Illustrated by Sharon Rentta

SCHOLASTIC INC.

New York Toronto London Auckland Sydney
Mexico City New Delhi Hong Kong Buenos Aires

ANIMAL MAGIC
Meet the animals

Visit our Web site at
www.animalmagicrescue.net

Working our
magic to match
the perfect pet
with the perfect
owner!

BRUNO
A golden Labrador, male,
about four years old.
Bruno is a nice dog
who likes people.

LOTTIE
This two-year-old cairn
terrier is a bundle of fun!
Lottie loves children and
would like to come
out to play!

JOEY
Joey the greyhound is
too old to race. He
would love a comfy,
quiet home where he
can dream of rabbits.

RESCUE CENTER
in need of a home!

ANIMAL RESCUE

GUINEVERE AND MERLIN
Mother and foal require a
new home together.
Guinevere can be ridden in
company and alone at all
paces. Good in traffic.

DOUGAL
An active and energetic
Dalmatian with lots of
character. Can you keep
up with this playful guy?

SUGAR AND SPICE
Sugar and Spice are
orphaned kittens. They're
ready to go to new owners
and would like a
home together.

SAGE AND THYME
Two more orphaned
kittens are looking for a
friendly new home. Can
you give them
the love they need?

Chapter One

"Almost there!" Eva called to her brother, Karl.

Karl was climbing a tree to rescue Tigger, a tabby cat who had managed to get himself stuck.

"Climb to your right—a bit farther," Eva instructed. "Yes, now try!"

Karl eased himself along a branch closer to Tigger. He reached out with one hand.

"Careful!" Tigger's owner, Ms. Eliot, warned.

She held her hands to her mouth, hardly daring to look.

"That's it, you're nearly there." Jimmy Harrison, Karl and Eva's grandfather, urged his grandson on.

The cat cowered on the branch. His yellow eyes glinted.

"Come here, Tigger!" Karl called softly.

He stretched as far as he dared.

Down below, Eva, their granddad, and Ms. Eliot watched anxiously.

"Don't you worry," Jimmy told Ms. Eliot. "We'll have Tigger down soon."

"That's good," Karl whispered as the cat stretched out a paw. "Come on, Tigger."

Tigger inched forward, his tail between his legs. Finally, Karl reached out and caught him.

"Great!" Eva said, as Karl clasped the cat to himself and began to climb down.

"Oh, my!" Ms. Eliot smiled with relief.

Jimmy Harrison grinned at his elderly neighbor. "I told you Karl could do it! Now all you have to do is open up a can of food and give him his supper. And while you're at it, you can have a nice cup of tea!"

As their granddad and the old woman disappeared inside the big house, Eva welcomed Karl and Tigger back to earth.

"Nice one!" She grinned at her brother, taking the cat from him while he brushed himself off.

"Animal Magic at your service, ma'am!" he laughed.

"Yeah, whatever. Anyway, I'm glad Granddad thought to call us. Ms. Eliot was ready to call the fire department!"

"Hmmm . . . It's a good thing Granddad lives next door," Karl muttered. Looking up at Ms. Eliot's big house, Karl could see paint peeling from the window frames and ivy choking the broken gutters. "Ash Tree Manor is one gigantic house for an old person living by herself."

Eva nodded, then carried Tigger indoors. "Who's hungry?" she murmured.

The second he saw his food dish, Tigger leapt out of her arms. Soon he was munching happily.

"Thank you so much," Ms. Eliot told Eva and Karl. "It's a relief to have Tigger back safe and sound."

Eva and Karl blushed. Their granddad smiled proudly.

"Now I know why your rescue center is called Animal Magic," the old woman said, shedding a happy tear. "It's as if I waved a magic wand and you brought Tigger and me a happy ending. We simply can't thank you enough!"

"Okay, Bruno, lie still while I take a look at you." Veterinarian Heidi Harrison spoke gently to the golden Labrador on her examination table.

Eva and Karl had raced back from Ash Tree Manor and burst in on their mom's examining room, eager to tell her the exciting Tigger rescue story.

The injured dog whimpered and stared up at Heidi with his deep brown eyes.

Joel Allerton, Heidi's assistant, stood close by. "Slow down," he said. "This poor guy's had a nasty fall. He was found at the foot of a very high wall. It looks like he's torn a ligament."

Carefully, Heidi tested the movement in Bruno's shoulder joint. "Yes," she confirmed. "He's probably going to need surgery to fix it."

"What happened? Did somebody dump him?" Eva asked.

Joel nodded.

"Your dad found him on the outskirts of town where the railway bridge crosses the road. We think he got pushed over the edge and landed on the shoulder of the road."

"Will he be okay?" Suddenly their exciting story about rescuing Tigger didn't seem so important.

Her mom nodded. "He should be fine. He's been very lucky. There's a name tag on his collar, but no phone number. He's not microchipped, either, so it'll be hard to trace the owner."

"Poor Bruno!" Eva murmured. Inside, she boiled with anger that anyone could shove this beautiful dog off a bridge. She stood back as Joel prepared a painkilling injection.

The dog whimpered again and raised his head.

Karl frowned. "Can I enter him on the Web site?" he asked.

"Go ahead, put his description up," Heidi said. She took the syringe from Joel and stroked Bruno's ears. "'A golden Lab, male, about four years old. Bruno is a nice dog who likes people.'"

Nodding, Karl disappeared into the office and sat at the computer. He typed quickly, then came back to take a photo of Bruno to put on the site.

"Where's Dad?" Eva asked.

"Outside, putting the finishing touches on

the stables," her mom told her. "Can't you hear him hammering?"

Yes, the stables! The very word cheered Eva up.

Animal Magic was about to open its doors to bigger unwanted animals such as horses, ponies, and goats, as well as to the dogs, cats, and rabbits they already looked after. A team of volunteers had given their time to convert a shed in the corner of the old farmyard. By this time next week the stables would be ready.

"I'll go and help!" she decided, escaping from the examining room and running across the yard to join her dad.

Chapter Two

All that evening and the next day, Eva worked in the new stables with her dad. She used a screwdriver to fix bolts on doors and a hammer to nail planks of wood to a partition wall.

"Good job," her dad told her before he left for work the following morning. "Tonight I'll pick up the bales of straw I ordered from Tom Ingleby's farm. You can come with me if you like."

"Yes, please." Eva always enjoyed a visit to

Tom's place. High Trees Farm was on the edge of town, and Tom owned the fields behind Animal Magic.

Eva hammered on. "How's Bruno?" she asked Joel when he popped his head over the stable door.

"The surgery went well," Joel replied. "His shoulder should heal within a few days."

"That's great news." Eva knew that Karl had already gotten two inquiries about Bruno on the Web site. "At this rate, we'll get him better and find him a new home before the end of our midterm vacation."

"Another success story," Joel grinned. "We're working our magic . . ."

". . . to match the perfect pet . . ."

". . . with the perfect owner!" Joel and Eva chanted the Animal Magic slogan.

Eva put down her hammer and stood back. "Time for a break," she decided.

"Want to help me pick up our bulk order of cat food from the Red Barn?" Joel asked.

"Cool. I'll just let Mom know." She followed him out to the yard, trying to creep past Mrs. Brooks next door without attracting attention.

But Linda Brooks looked up from planting a neat row of red and white flowers along the side of her lawn.

"How's Annie doing in Devon?" Eva asked about her best friend, who was on vacation with her cousins.

"Fine, thank you, Eva," came the brisk reply. Mrs. Brooks peeled off her gardening gloves and came up to the wall. "Joel, I'd like a word with you if you can spare a moment."

"Sure. What can I do for you, Linda?"

"You can pass on a message, please. I'd like you to tell Heidi to expect a visit from the Town Council."

Joel and Eva exchanged worried looks.

"Jason and I have lodged our petition at the Town Hall," Mrs. Brooks explained. "We gathered signatures of people opposing Animal Magic on the grounds of excessive animal noise and car traffic, and I delivered the petition to the Council office on Monday morning."

"Good for you, Linda," Joel muttered under his breath.

Eva could hardly bear to listen. *This is the countryside!* she thought. *Animals live in the country. You expect them to make noise!* She couldn't believe that Annie's parents had actually gone ahead and done what they'd been threatening to do ever since Animal Magic opened a year ago.

"So you'll inform Heidi?" Linda asked stiffly. Joel nodded. Mrs. Brooks gave a triumphant smile before turning on her heel and going back to her gardening.

Joel sighed and hung his head. "Come on, Eva, let's forget the cat food," he muttered. "I'd better pass this news on to your mom before I lose control and leap over that fence to tear up Linda's precious flower bed!"

"I've been expecting it," Heidi admitted when Eva and Joel gave her Mrs. Brooks's message. She was in the clinic, busy with a new arrival, a cat who was still inside a wicker carrier, meowing to be let out.

"Mrs. Brooks is so mean!" Eva cried. "She's asking the Council to close us down without even thinking about what would happen to all our animals!"

"I know." Over the months, Heidi had gotten used to her neighbor's constant complaints and threats. Even now she was determined not to let it upset her. "Let's not think about that now, Eva. Why don't you open up the carrier and help me take a look at this little guy."

"What if Animal Magic has to close?" Eva demanded, unbuckling the leather strap. "Where will all our animals go?"

"Not now, Eva. Joel, we'll need to prepare a new cage in the cat kennels. Can you go and make sure there's food and water?" Eva opened the carrier and Heidi reached inside, lifting out a wary tabby cat with staring yellow eyes.

"Hey, that's Tigger!" Eva recognized him right away. She ran to the door and called

Karl, who was busy cleaning his bike in the yard. "Karl, come and look. Ms. Eliot's tabby has been brought in!"

"What happened?" Karl asked, his forehead damp under his floppy dark bangs. He'd just cycled to Okeham and back with his friend George Stevens.

"Hey, Tigger!" Eva murmured, petting his soft, striped fur. "What's happened to Ms. Eliot?" she asked her mom.

"Better ask your granddad," Heidi answered, beginning to examine the new arrival. "He brought Tigger in half an hour ago."

"Let's ride over there," Karl said in a hurry, hardly waiting for Eva to grab her bike and follow.

Eva and Karl pedaled hard along Main Street toward their grandfather's garden center on the edge of Okeham. Soon they

saw the large green-and-white Gro-well
sign and the long rows of greenhouses,
where Jimmy Harrison grew and sold his
plants.

"Granddad, how come you brought
Tigger to the rescue center?" Karl asked,
charging into the shop.

Eva was right behind him. "What happened to Ms. Eliot? Is she okay?"

Jimmy, who was potting small green seedlings into larger pots, looked over the rim of his glasses. "Ah, yes. Not good news, I'm afraid," he murmured. "I found poor Ms. Eliot collapsed on her kitchen floor this morning. I had to call for an ambulance."

"Did she go to the hospital?" Eva gasped.

Her granddad nodded. "I don't know how long she'll be there, but she asked me to take care of her animals."

Karl fiddled with the plastic plant labels on the counter. "Animals—plural?"

"I thought Tigger was the only one," Eva cut in.

"Tigger is the only *cat*," her granddad agreed. "And it was easy enough for me to drop him off at your place."

"But?" Karl prompted.

"But Guinevere is more of a problem," Jimmy admitted. "I've already phoned your dad, and he's coming over as soon as he can."

"Guinevere?" Eva stared at the tall gray house next door. "Who's she?"

"Come and see," their granddad invited. He led the way down the side of the greenhouse and through a narrow gate into a field beyond. "I couldn't exactly fit this fine lady into the back of my Land Rover!"

The green field sloped gently toward a stream where a row of willow trees grew. As Eva and Karl took in their new surroundings, they saw a large gray shape in the shadow of the overhanging branches.

"Wow, is that a pony?" Karl exclaimed.

Eva's mouth fell open. Sure enough, a beautiful dapple gray pony emerged from the trees. Her mane and tail were pure white. She trod heavily up the hill toward them.

"Meet Guinevere," their granddad announced. "This is Ms. Eliot's gray mare. And as you can see, she's about to give birth to a foal any day now!"

Chapter Three

"She's gorgeous!" Eva breathed, watching her dad and granddad begin to load the gray mare into a trailer that Mark had borrowed from Tom Ingleby.

Guinevere's mane was silky soft, and her dappled coat shone in the sunlight.

"Take good care of her," Jimmy Harrison said. "Remember, I promised Ms. Eliot that her pony would get five-star treatment!"

"Looks like we'll have to open the

stables early," Karl said. "Should I go ahead and make sure everything's ready?"

His dad nodded. "I dropped off the bales of straw on the way here. Eva, you go with your brother and make a nice deep bed in the stall closest to the door, okay?"

As Karl rode off, Eva lingered to see her dad lead Guinevere safely up the ramp into the trailer. Then she set off, pedaling hard until she reached home.

"Mom," she yelled, "Dad's bringing a pony! She's having a foal! We have to lay straw in the stable for her!"

Heidi stood in the doorway to the clinic. "I know. Karl already told me. It's exciting, isn't it?"

"Totally. She's beautiful, Mom. Just wait till you see her!" Flinging her bike down, Eva raced into the stables, where she found Karl cutting through string that tied the bales of straw. She dived in and took an armful, scattering it on the floor. "How cool is this!"

"Calm down," Karl grunted. "Look at you—you're covered in straw."

"I don't care. We're getting a pony!" Eva's dark eyes shone. Suddenly, she stared at Karl. "Hey, do you think the foal will be born while Guinevere's here?"

"It depends how long Ms. Eliot has to stay in the hospital," Karl pointed out.

"The pony did look pretty pregnant, didn't she?" Eva said eagerly.

"Oh, so now you're an expert, are you?" As usual, Karl tried not to let his feelings show.

"I bet she has the foal here!" Eva insisted. "How cool will that be?"

At the sound of their dad's van, they

both ran out into the yard. They helped
him slide the bolts at the back of the trailer
and then lower the ramp.

"Let's take a look at the mother to be,"
Heidi said, coming forward to examine
Guinevere before they unloaded her. "Oh,
yes, it's going to be any day now. Bring
her out gently. Keep her nice and calm."

Eva held her breath as her dad led
Guinevere down the ramp. "Her stall's
ready," she said, holding the door open.

"Easy, girl," Mark said. He waited for the
mare to take in her new surroundings.

She stood in the doorway, looking this
way and that. Her ears were pricked and
she swished her tail. Then she must have
decided that her new home was good
enough, because she stepped forward onto
the fresh straw bed and let out a long,
satisfied whinny.

"Guinevere needs peace and quiet," Heidi told Eva. "When a mare is about to give birth, the last thing she wants is people petting her and fussing."

"But how will we know when it's happening?" Eva asked.

"We may not. It often happens in the middle of the night, quite naturally, without any help from us."

Eva nodded. "So we come out in the morning and the foal is here, already tottering around on its wobbly legs!" She pictured the magical moment.

"Fingers crossed," Heidi said. "So what I'm saying is, leave Guinevere alone for a while. How about taking a dog for a walk instead?"

Eva nodded and went to fetch Dougal from the kennels. As she went in she was greeted by a chorus of woofs and barks.

"Hey, Sam. Hey, Lottie. Hey, Millie," she said as she passed each kennel, saying hello to a retriever, a cairn terrier, and a cocky crossbreed.

"Your turn for a walk, Dougal," she told the cute Dalmatian.

Dougal loved his runs along the riverbank, and when he saw the leash in Eva's hand he went crazy with delight.

"Down!" she told him sternly. "Heel!" she said as she got him on the leash.

They left the kennels, crossed the yard, and went down an alley toward the river, where Eva let Dougal off the leash.

Off he dashed. He sniffed at the entrance to a rabbit burrow, then ran through the long grass with just the tip of his white tail showing.

"Dougal, come back!" Eva cried as the playful Dalmatian made a sharp detour over a narrow stone bridge toward Okeham's golf course.

Luckily, he obeyed and came bounding back to Eva. On the far side of the river, a group of golfers gathered on a smooth green. Eva recognized Jason Brooks, their next-door neighbor.

"Heel, Dougal!" she murmured, glad that she and Karl had spent time training him not to run off. He even ignored the two fishermen sitting on the riverbank, who surprised Eva by standing up and yelling at her to clear off.

Eva frowned. She didn't like the look of the two men, who seemed to be angry without good reason. "Come here, Dougal. Heel!" she called again.

Obediently, Dougal walked to heel, tail and head up, as they headed away from the river along a footpath beside one of the fields belonging to Tom Ingleby. The footpath brought them back to Main Street, where Eva put Dougal on the leash and walked him home. "Good boy!" she said with a grin, thinking that he looked like a pirate, with a big black patch over one eye.

Dougal wagged his long tail and trotted into the kennels, where Eva settled him down for the night.

"Good night, Joey. Good night, Trixie," she murmured, passing a greyhound and a Jack Russell.

The dogs yapped and wagged their tails. As Eva turned off the light and closed the door, they fell silent.

She crossed the yard and went into the

house, where she found Karl at his computer, updating the Animal Magic Web site.

"Hi, Eva. A woman is coming to look at Dougal tomorrow," he reported.

"Cool. Where are Mom and Dad?"

"In their room."

Eva heard the low voices of her parents from across the landing. "The Town Council is sending someone to see us tomorrow afternoon," Heidi was saying. "They didn't give an exact time."

"Do you want me to be here?" Mark asked.

"No, there's no point. It's only a quick visit. I can tell them everything they need to know."

Eva gasped. "Did you hear that?" she hissed at Karl, who nodded.

"Let's hope they don't take Linda's side," Mark went on. "We could be in serious trouble if they do."

There was a long pause. "It will mean that all our work at Animal Magic will have to stop," Heidi admitted. "The Council could close us down overnight!"

Eva lay awake late that night worrying. Every time she closed her eyes she pictured a man from the Council signing a piece of paper saying that Animal Magic had to close.

Then who would find a home for Bruno once his shoulder had healed, or for Joey the greyhound who was too old to race anymore? Who would look after animals like Tigger and Guinevere while their owners were in the hospital?

Eva tossed and turned. It was no good— she couldn't sleep even if it was two o'clock in the morning! Getting out of bed, she crept to her window, opened it, and listened to the silence. In the distance there was the low hoot of an owl.

I wonder how Guinevere is doing? she thought, looking over at the stables. She listened in the darkness and after a few moments was sure she could hear restless movements coming from the stables—the sound of the pony's feet rustling through dry straw, a low snort, the knock of a hoof against a wooden door. It was no good. Whatever her mom had said about Guinevere needing peace and quiet, Eva had to go and take a look!

Chapter Four

Eva found Guinevere standing in her bed of straw. She tossed her head in the low glimmer of a safety lamp fixed high on the wall.

"Hey, girl!" Eva murmured. She watched anxiously as the mare began to pace to and fro, then folded her knees and went down on her side, only to get up and pace again. "Take it easy," Eva breathed.

But Guinevere was restless. She rustled

through the straw, went down again, rolled onto her other side, and was back on her feet.

"I guess it's time for your foal to be born," Eva whispered, feeling sure she was right. She didn't move.

Guinevere went down on her side a third time, and stayed. Her wide sides heaved as she laid her head on the straw.

"Oh!" Eva was scared. Guinevere looked agitated and helpless. Would it be okay to go right into the stall with her?

The mare lifted her head from the straw. She rolled her eyes.

"You're doing fine!" Eva murmured.

There were footsteps outside, and Heidi came into the stall. "I couldn't sleep, either. I heard you come down," she muttered to Eva. She took one look at the mare. "Yes, this is it!"

She went into the stable and knelt
down by Guinevere's side to test her
pulse. Then she held a stethoscope to
the mare's belly. "Uh-oh, the foal's
heartbeat isn't very strong. I think
Guinevere will need help to deliver it,"
she decided. "Eva, Joel's on night duty.
Run to the clinic and get him."

Nodding, Eva ran off. She found Joel feeding a litter of orphaned kittens with milk from plastic droppers. "Guinevere . . . foal . . . come quick!" she gasped.

Together they ran back to the stables.

"Okay, this is happening faster than I expected," Heidi warned. "The foal's head has already emerged. Joel, help me ease it out. Eva, you stay where you are."

Anxiously, Eva watched her mom and Joel assist Guinevere. She saw the new foal emerge and slither gently onto the straw.

"Don't panic, it's all over!" Heidi said, glancing up at Eva.

"Is she—are *they* okay?" Eva asked.

Heidi's eyes were bright. "Come and see."

Eva tiptoed toward Guinevere's stall and looked in.

"I had to turn the foal's head and help him out," Heidi said. "He was stuck for a while back there."

He? The foal was a he! Eva held her breath. And there he was—the smallest, youngest, skinniest, shakiest foal she'd ever seen!

The baby lay in the straw. His mother licked him clean and then nudged him with her nose. He braced his front legs and tried to push himself up.

"His head is enormous!" Eva exclaimed. "And his legs are so skinny!"

Guinevere nudged and shoved him gently from behind. The foal was gray, like her, with big dark eyes.

He tried to stand once more. He got up, tottered, fell over, and tried again.

"Ah!" Eva gasped. "How smart is that!"

"That's what they're programmed to do," Heidi told her quietly. "In the wild, they have to be up on their feet and running away from danger almost the minute they're born!"

And now the foal was standing on his shaky legs, and Guinevere was licking him clean, and he was turning to her and beginning to suckle.

"That is so-o-o magical!" Eva murmured. "Guinevere, you're amazing!"

"Would you like to give him a name?"

her mom asked, smiling at Joel.

Eva gazed at the suckling foal. "Let's call him Merlin," she whispered. "Like the wizard. 'Cause he's magic!"

"So, Ms. Eliot, you'll be pleased to know that your mare has had her foal," Jimmy Harrison said.

He had brought Karl and Eva to visit the old woman in the hospital just after lunch the following day. She looked pale and thin, propped up on pillows, with bedsheets folded neatly under her chin.

"He's gray, like his mom," Eva broke in. "His mane sticks straight up, and he's got the longest legs. I was there when he was born!"

"Slow down," Karl warned. "Sorry, Eva's always butting in."

Ms. Eliot smiled weakly. "Not at all. You're excited, aren't you, dear? And so am I. I was looking forward to seeing the birth myself, but it wasn't meant to be."

"Merlin got up on his feet right away!" Eva exclaimed.

"Merlin?" Ms. Eliot interrupted.

Eva blushed. "Oh, Mom said I could give him a name—just for now—so I chose Merlin."

"What a good choice! I think he should keep it. And how is my lovely Guinevere?"

"Mom says she's doing well," Karl reported. "And so is Tigger. He's happy in the cat kennels."

Ms. Eliot nodded and then turned her head toward Jimmy. "The doctors tell me I had a slight stroke—nothing too serious, but it's given me a shock."

"You'll have to take it easy from now on," Jimmy told her kindly. "When you get back home, I'll pop in and keep an eye on you, don't you worry."

Tears appeared in Ms. Eliot's eyes. She shook her head and they trickled down her lined cheeks. "I'm afraid I won't be coming home, Mr. Harrison."

"Well, not yet," he conceded. "But in a while, when you're stronger."

"Not ever," the old woman told him faintly. "I have to face facts and admit that Ash Tree Manor is too much for me now."

Jimmy was about to protest, but Ms. Eliot shook her head.

"I've lived in the old house all my life, and I shall always have many wonderful memories of my time there. But now I've made up my mind to sell it and move into an apartment," Ms. Eliot announced. "Tigger will be able to come with me, but not the ponies, of course."

Eva gasped in alarm. *This can't be happening!* she thought. She stared at Ms. Eliot's sad face.

"I would like your son and daughter-in-law to find a wonderful new home for Guinevere and her foal," Ms. Eliot insisted. "I would be so grateful to them if they succeed."

Chapter Five

"Guinevere and Merlin." Karl added the ponies' names to the Animal Magic Web site at the reception desk in the clinic. He remembered what Ms. Eliot had told him. "Mother and foal need a new home together. Guinevere can be ridden in company and alone at all paces. Good in traffic. Merlin needs to be with his mom."

"Listen to this," Karl called out to Eva. "Does it sound okay?"

She listened carefully as he read the new posting out loud. "You've used two *needs*," she pointed out.

"Okay, Ms. Fussy, I'll change the first *need* to *require*." Karl nodded, then worked on. "I'll be out to take photos in a couple of minutes," he muttered. "Can you get Guinevere and Merlin ready?"

"What do you mean?" Eva asked.

"You know, brushing and grooming. Horsey stuff." Karl pretended that he didn't know or care much about it, but really he was as much in love with the mare and her foal as everyone else. Every time he looked at Merlin, his heart melted.

"Give me five minutes," Eva replied, dashing out to the stables. Once there, she slowed down, moving quietly around the ponies as she mucked out their stall, laid fresh straw, and then took a brush to

Guinevere's long mane.

The mare stood patiently, keeping one watchful eye on her foal, who tottered unsteadily through the new straw.

"He's gorgeous, isn't he?" Eva murmured, smiling at Merlin's wobbly legs and soft, tufty tail. She couldn't believe how tiny his hooves were, or how big his eyes and ears seemed. And he wasn't scared of having her in the stall with them. Instead, he came close and took a nip at the hem of Eva's T-shirt.

"Hey!" she protested with a smile. She turned and let him take a good sniff at her boots and jeans.

Then Guinevere nudged Eva from behind, as if to say, "You haven't finished yet." Eva turned back to Guinevere and was just giving her mane a final brush when someone opened the stable door.

"Nearly finished," she called out, expecting Karl.

But it was her mom who interrupted. "Eva, this is Mr. Winters. He's come from the Council to take a look at us."

Eva frowned and chewed her lip. In the excitement of Merlin's birth, she'd forgotten all about Linda Brooks's petition and the visit from the Council. She mumbled hello.

"We've just opened the stables," Heidi explained to their visitor. "Guinevere and Merlin are our first customers. I'm hoping to give shelter to goats, ponies, and donkeys before finding them new owners. I also plan to link up with Leebank Pony Sanctuary to find a permanent place for those animals we can't find homes for."

"So you don't intend to keep any large animals here long-term?" Mr. Winters checked. He was a small, stout man wearing a gray suit and a red-and-gray striped tie. He was carrying a blue folder and seemed to be taking lots of notes.

Eva continued grooming Guinevere as her mom led Mr. Winters outside.

"No, but we do expect this section of the center to be busy, just like the kennels," Heidi answered honestly. "In fact, to be frank, Mr. Winters, we're already bursting at the seams."

Eva sighed as the voices faded. She stroked Guinevere's neck. "You hear that? Mr. Winters is checking up on us to see if we're too noisy."

Guinevere dipped her head and snorted.

"Exactly!" Eva agreed. "That's what I think. And Merlin thinks so, too!" She pressed her lips together and made a *puh* sound. *Too noisy? What a load of garbage!*

Eva caught sight of Mr. Winters again on his way out. As she left the stables, he was shaking hands with her mom, but his face gave nothing away. Was he happy with what he'd seen or not?

Heidi sighed and shook her head as she turned and walked back into the office. Eva

was about to follow when she saw Linda
Brooks greet Mr. Winters on the sidewalk.

"Ah, Mr. Winters!" she called. "I'm glad
you followed up on my letter of complaint
and my petition. Now you can see for
yourself how difficult it is for the residents
of Okeham to have this animal rescue
center in our midst!"

Mr. Winters's reply was too low for Eva
to hear, but as she stood watching, Jason
Brooks's car pulled into the driveway
next door, and Annie jumped out of the
car.

"Hey, Eva!" Annie cried, dumping her
vacation bag and running
into the yard. "Wow, am
I glad to be back!
How are you?
What's new at
Animal Magic?"

"Annie, come and say hi to your mom!" Jason Brooks called in vain. He hurried over to his wife's side just as Mr. Winters escaped Linda Brooks's clutches and drove off.

Annie looked tan. Her usually neat hair was flying in all directions.

"How was Devon?" Eva asked.

"Cool. I rode ponies and swam in the sea every day. But what's happening here? What's with the long face?"

"That was only a visit from the Council to see if your mom can get us closed down!" Eva muttered. But she couldn't stay glum for long. "Never mind, it's not your fault, Annie. And guess what—we have a new foal. Come and look!"

"Annie!" Jason Brooks called after her.

"I won't be long!" she yelled as Eva dragged her into the stables.

"Ah!" Annie's eyes lit up when she saw Merlin.

He was nestled in the deep straw, his long legs folded beneath him. He looked up at the two girls and blinked sleepily.

"How cute is he!" Annie breathed. "Can I go in and pet him?"

Eva nodded. She led Annie into the stall. "Is this okay?" she asked Guinevere, who hovered close to where her foal lay.

The mare lowered her head and made way for Eva and Annie.

Annie knelt down next to Merlin and reached out to stroke him. "He's so soft!"

"He can stand and walk already!" Eva said, kneeling next to Annie.

Annie could hardly speak through her broad smile. "What's his name?"

"Merlin," Eva whispered.

Annie gave a soft laugh as Merlin nuzzled her hand. "And what's he doing here at Animal Magic?" she asked.

"He and his mom need a new home," Eva explained. "Hey, I don't suppose you know anyone who lives in a house surrounded by fields—someone who loves horses and has space to take in two more?"

Annie sat back. She thought for a while, then answered, "Actually, Eva, I do!"

Chapter Six

"Devon?" Karl asked.

The family was discussing Guinevere and Merlin's future over supper that night. Eva had told them about Annie's pony-loving cousins by the sea.

"I know. It's miles away," Eva said. "But Annie's sure her aunt and uncle would take them. They already own a horse and a pony. And they have lots of space."

"But we'd never see them again," Karl pointed out.

"What's the family's name?" their dad asked thoughtfully.

Eva recalled the details that Annie had given her. "Simmons. There's her Aunt Ruth and Uncle David, plus Annie's two cousins, Jess and Molly. They live on a farm overlooking the sea."

"So that must be Linda's sister and her husband." Heidi worked it out as she collected the dirty dishes and put them in the dishwasher.

Eva traced patterns on the tablecloth with an extra fork. "What do you think, Mom? Is it a good idea?"

Heidi turned to Karl. "Have we had any replies to the posting on the Web site?"

He shook his head. "But it's only been up there for a day. Anyway, I think we should say no to Annie's idea. Devon is too far away."

"I know how you feel, but I think we should check it out," his dad argued. "Look at it from Guinevere and Merlin's point of view. A home by the seaside with other horses – it sounds perfect!"

"What else did Annie say?" Heidi asked Eva.

"She said her Aunt Ruth and her mom used to ride all the time when they were kids. Ruth is still a real animal lover, and Jess and Molly are, too." Reluctantly, Eva spoke the truth. Like Karl, she longed to find somewhere closer for Guinevere and Merlin.

Frowning moodily, Karl stood up from the table. "It's a stupid idea. What will Ms. Eliot say? She'll have to say good-bye to Guinevere and never see her again. That's not fair!"

"Right!" Eva agreed, sorely regretting that

she'd mentioned the Devon idea. She looked from her mom to her dad, then back again.

"We need to talk to Ms. Eliot," Mark pointed out. "After all, it will be her decision in the end."

"Meanwhile, I'll call Leebank Pony Sanctuary and arrange a visit," Heidi said. "You never know—perhaps they'll have room for a mare and foal."

"I'll come!" Eva cried, grabbing onto her mom's new idea.

"Me, too!" Karl volunteered.

Please let it be Leebank, not Devon! Eva wished as she left the house and made a beeline for the stables. *Better still, let it be Animal Magic forever!*

How cool would that be! Guinevere and Merlin could live in Tom Ingleby's field at the back of their rescue center. And every

morning Eva would get up and go down to
the field to see the dapple gray mare and
her gorgeous foal. They would look up at
her and whinny. She would greet them and
they would trot through the lush green
grass toward her.

Hey, she would even buy a saddle for
Guinevere and learn to ride. Merlin would
tag along until he was old enough to be
trained.

But in her heart Eva knew it wouldn't happen that way. No. Animal Magic would find a new home for the wonderful duo, and Eva's dream would end.

"Merlin is a newborn—he's just one day old," Heidi explained to Cath Brown, the owner of Leebank Pony Sanctuary the following morning. "We need to find a new home for him. Of course, we won't move him anywhere until he's a good deal older."

"Right." Cath nodded. "And you'll need to find someone who will keep him with his mother for the first year or so, until he's weaned and ready to leave her."

Eva and Karl sat in the back of their mom's car, listening to the grown-ups talk. "I like it here!" Eva muttered.

Karl grunted. He didn't dare to hope that Leebank would become Guinevere and Merlin's new home—that would be too good to be true.

"No, honestly. Look at all the horses and ponies in the fields!"

Leebank sat in a valley with a stream running through it. The yard overlooked three big fields full of grazing animals.

"Fifteen, sixteen, seventeen," Karl counted. "Twenty-two altogether."

Meanwhile, Eva concentrated on Cath Brown, a tall, sturdy woman dressed in a blue quilted jacket, jeans, and boots.

"I'm very happy to set up a link with Animal Magic," Cath was telling Heidi. "For instance, if people bring horses and ponies to me who are in need of a vet, I can bring them over to you for treatment. Likewise, if you need to find a home for a pony and you've tried everywhere else without success, then I can provide a home here as a last resort."

"Look at that big brown-and-white one!" Karl nudged Eva and pointed to a horse who had come up to the gate.

Eva couldn't resist. She got out of the car and went to stroke the horse. He had thick, feathered legs and a long white mane that fell forward over his face. He was so hairy he even had a funny, curled mustache at the end of his nose.

"What's his name?" Eva called to Cath.

"That's Major. He's thirty-three years old." Cath came over with a carrot for the elderly horse.

"Wow!" Eva couldn't get over Major's size and hairiness. "What do you think about Guinevere and Merlin?" she asked.

Cath smiled. "They sound great. And

Guinevere sounds as if she's taken to motherhood, no problem."

"Merlin is so perfect!" Eva told her.

"And you're longing to keep him?" Cath guessed.

Major's mustache wobbled up and down as he ate his carrot.

"Yeah, but we can't." Eva sighed, enjoying the sight of other ponies ambling up the fields toward them. "Can you?" she asked suddenly, keeping her fingers crossed behind her back.

Cath sighed. "Like I said, Leebank is a last resort. And your mom says there's a chance of Guinevere and Merlin being sent to a good home in Devon."

"Miles and miles away!" Eva protested.

"But they would do well there—on a farm with other animals, and with kids to ride them."

"*I* could ride them if they lived here," Eva
pleaded. She felt her hopes fade as Cath
smiled sympathetically.

"Send them to Devon," Cath advised.
"They'll have a good life down there."

Chapter Seven

"Okay, so we have two people interested in Guinevere." As soon as they got back from the pony sanctuary, Karl went into the reception area and checked the Web site. "One says she can't take Merlin, though."

"We can't split them up!" Eva insisted, reading the e-mails over her brother's shoulder. "And look, this other one's the opposite. They want the foal, but not the mare. What's wrong with them? Don't they read the postings properly?"

"Hi, Annie, any news from Devon?" Heidi asked, looking up from her examination of Bruno when Eva's friend appeared. Late morning clinic hours had ended, and all was quiet at Animal Magic.

"Aunt Ruth says she'll definitely think about giving Guinevere and Merlin a home," Annie replied cautiously just as the phone began to ring. "But she can't give you an answer right away."

Eva frowned. Right now, with Leebank only to be used as a last resort and no other offers, Devon looked like the only choice.

"Answer the phone, would you, Eva?" Heidi muttered as she checked out movement in Bruno's injured shoulder.

Eva reached for the receiver.

"Hi, this is Cath Brown from Leebank," the voice said. "Is this Eva?"

"Yes, do you want to speak to Mom?"

"No. Can you just give her a quick message? I forgot to mention one important thing when you dropped by, which is that the police stopped by here about a week ago to warn me that two horse thieves are operating in the area. I thought you should know, since it'll be time to put your mare and foal out to pasture soon. When you do, make sure the field is secure."

"Okay, thanks." The message worried Eva. For a moment she wondered if the two angry fishermen she'd seen while walking Dougal had anything to do with the horse thieves. But when she told her mom, Heidi had good news.

"Don't worry, your dad worked out a deal with Tom Ingleby earlier today. Tom has promised to rent us his field facing onto the golf course for as long as we need it. You know, the one you can see from your house, Annie."

"Hey, neat!" Annie grinned. "I'll be able to look out my bedroom window and see Guinevere and Merlin!"

"So?" Eva prompted her mom, trying not to feel jealous.

"So, there's no direct access to that field from the main road," Heidi explained. "In other words, no horse thief can drive a trailer anywhere near Guinevere and Merlin when we put them out there tomorrow morning."

Reassured, Eva went off with Annie to feed the orphaned kittens in the cat kennels. As they passed by Tigger's cage, Ms. Eliot's tabby gave a loud meow.

"What a gorgeous cat!" Annie said.

"He's going back to his owner as soon as

she's out of the hospital, so don't get any ideas about adopting him," Eva kidded.

Annie sighed. "As if! You know what Mom's like!"

"I sure do!" Eva raised her eyebrows. Soon she and Annie were busy with the four tiny kittens, dropping milk into their greedy pink mouths.

The kittens squirmed and swallowed, curling their tongues around the plastic tube and sucking out every drop.

"So, you get to see Merlin out your window and I don't," Eva sighed. Her bedroom overlooked the yard and the office.

"Yeah, but you got to see him being born!" Annie reminded her. "And you can pet him whenever you like! I can't believe he feels so soft!"

"As soft as these kittens," Eva said. They were finished with the feeding, so she and Annie nestled the orphans down in their warm bed and left the cat kennels. "Do you want to take a peek at Merlin before you go?" she asked.

Annie glanced at her watch. "I promised Mom I'd be back at one—but hey, she won't mind if I'm a few minutes late!"

Eva led the way into the stables. "Hush!" she murmured, raising a finger to her lips.

Merlin was resting in the straw. Guinevere raised her head as the girls drew close and peered into the stall.

"Oh, he's so cool!" Annie breathed. "And skinny! And cute!"

Eva nodded happily. "Can we come in?" she asked Guinevere, gently opening the door and motioning Annie in after her. "The first thing I thought after he was born was, 'Wow, how skinny!'" she confessed. "Then I saw him stand up on these long, wobbly legs, and I thought he'd never be able to do it, but Guinevere nudged him and he got up and he stood there trembling all over!"

"Is it okay to pet him again?" Annie checked. "Oh, he's so gorgeous! Look, he's standing up!"

Jerkily getting to his feet, Merlin shook himself and then tottered toward Eva. He pushed his soft nose against her arm and then gave a small hop and skip toward Annie.

"He likes me!" Annie smiled. But just as she reached out to stroke him, she heard her mother's voice calling and drawing nearer. "Uh-oh, I should have known!" With a start she drew back, making Guinevere glance anxiously toward the stable door.

"Annie, where are you? I warned you not to be late for lunch," Linda Brooks called.

"In here, Mom!" Annie replied softly, wiping her hands on her jeans as she backed out of the stall.

Linda appeared in the door, her forehead creased by a deep frown. But when she spotted Guinevere and her tiny foal, for a moment her face softened.

"Oh, my!" she murmured before the hard mask returned. She cleared her throat. "Annie, come along. Your lunch is getting cold!"

Blushing, Annie joined her mom, who sneaked one final look at Merlin before she turned and marched away.

"Did you see that?" Eva muttered as she patted Guinevere's neck. "For a second back there I thought Mrs. Brooks was about to crack a smile!"

The gray mare nuzzled at Eva's pockets.

"Sorry, no treats!" Eva smiled. "But listen, Guinnie, there was this look on Annie's mom's face, all soft and gooey, like everyone else when they first set eyes on Merlin. I was so surprised!"

This really made Eva think. She knelt down in the straw beside the foal, who cozied up to be petted. "Of course, she switched it off quickly, but I did see it. And you know something?" she murmured, wrapping her arms around Merlin's neck. "The truth is, Linda Brooks fell in love with you on the spot."

Merlin turned his head and nuzzled Eva's shoulder.

Eva smiled. "She did," she insisted. "And you know something else? I've just had a totally brilliant idea!"

Chapter Eight

"Forget Devon!" Eva told Karl, brimming with confidence as she barged into his room.

Her brother was busy as usual updating the Web site. He sat with his back to her. "Sugar and Spice are orphaned kittens," he typed. "They're ready to go to new owners and would like a home together."

"I said, forget Devon for Guinevere and Merlin!" Eva insisted. "I've thought of something perfect!"

"So, impress me," Karl muttered, scanning in an image of the two black kittens.

"I'm serious, Karl!" Eva swiveled his chair away from his desk. "Listen, you'd like to find Merlin and Guinnie a home close to Okeham, wouldn't you?"

"It's not up to us," he said. "Everyone else thinks Devon is a good idea."

"Except Ms. Eliot!" Eva pointed out. "No one's told her yet. It's going to break her heart!"

Karl frowned. "You're only saying that because you want to keep them nearby so *you* can see them!"

"No, I'm not."

"Yes, you are."

"Well, maybe a little, but do you want to hear my idea or don't you?"

Karl turned back toward the screen. "Go

ahead. You're going to tell me anyway."

"Okay, this is it! Mrs. Brooks came to get Annie earlier, and she saw Merlin . . ."

"Sage and Thyme," Karl typed, his shoulders hunched, his back to Eva again. "Two more orphaned kittens are looking for a friendly new home . . ."

"Her face softened the moment she saw him!"

"So?"

"So, she's like everyone else—she's fallen in love with him!"

"So?" Karl muttered again.

"So, she used to go riding when she was young—Annie told me. She loves horses, even if she tries to pretend she doesn't!"

"Are we talking about Linda Brooks—as in the woman who just sent a petition to the Town Council to get us closed down?" Karl scoffed.

"Karl, listen. You didn't see her face when she set eyes on Merlin. She really liked him. So my idea is to get Linda to adopt him and Guinevere!"

Karl spun around in his seat, his eyes narrowed. "You're crazy!"

"I am not!"

"Yes, you are. You're always having wild ideas. Now let me work, okay?"

Eva gritted her teeth. "You wait!" she muttered, storming off to her own room. "I'm going to make it happen!"

The next morning, Eva was bringing Joey the greyhound back from a walk by the river when she bumped into Annie at the entrance to Animal Magic.

"Hey, Eva, I was looking for you," Annie greeted her, stooping to pat Joey. "I've got good news. Mom spoke to Aunt Ruth again about Guinevere and Merlin and the answer's yes!"

"Oh!" Eva walked on toward the kennels with Joey.

"Aren't you pleased?" Annie ran after her. "Isn't that what you wanted?"

Just then, Eva's granddad drove through the gates, and Karl came out of the house to say hello.

"How are my favorite grandkids?" Jimmy asked with a broad grin as he got out of his car.

"Granddad, we're your *only* grandkids!" Eva grinned back, handing Joey's leash to Annie, who had offered to put him back in his kennel.

"Exactly!" He gave her shoulder a quick squeeze. "I thought I'd come and check up on Tigger for Ms. Eliot."

"How is she?" Karl asked.

"Not too bad. She comes out of the hospital on Monday and will move into an apartment with an aide to keep an eye on her. The old house is already up for sale."

"Well, tell her Tigger's fine," Karl said.

"And we're pretty sure we've found a home for Guinevere and Merlin—in Devon."

"Yes, it's all set!" Annie announced, coming out onto the kennel porch.

Eva pressed her lips together and kept quiet, watching her granddad's reaction.

"Well, that's a long way away," Jimmy said, shaking his head. "I'm not sure how Ms. Eliot will feel about that."

"She'll hate it!" Eva broke in.

"But it's a good home," Annie insisted.

"I'd better tell Ms. Eliot, then. I hope it doesn't come as too much of a shock," Jimmy said, worried. He set off for the house to find Mark and Heidi.

Eva ran after him. "Don't tell Ms. Eliot about Devon just yet," she pleaded.

Her granddad turned to study her face. "Why? Do you have something else in mind?" he asked.

Eva's eyes were bright and eager. "Actually, yes!" she nodded. "I'm working on it. So don't worry, Granddad, I'm pretty sure I'll find Merlin and Guinevere a place *much* closer to home!"

"Meanwhile, it's business as usual," Heidi announced after she and Mark had finished telling Jimmy about the problem with the Council over a cup of coffee. Eva sat quietly in a corner of the kitchen, listening to their conversation.

"Did they say how long they'd take to make a decision?" Jimmy asked.

Mark shook his head. "But you know us, Dad—we always look on the bright side. There are lots of people in Okeham who support Animal Magic, in spite of the ones who signed Linda's petition."

"Why can't people like Linda Brooks see what a good job you're doing here?" Jimmy grumbled.

"Listen, we're not solving anything sitting here talking," Heidi decided, catching Eva's eye. "It's time to take Guinevere and Merlin out into the field for the first time. Eva, would you like to put a bridle on Guinevere and help me lead her out?"

The words were hardly out of her mom's mouth before Eva was halfway across the yard. She dashed into the stables.

"Guess what!" she told Guinevere, grabbing a bridle from its hook on the wall. "You're going outside!"

The mare stamped her feet and turned to edge Merlin toward the door.

Carefully, Eva strapped the bridle on and clipped a lead rope in place. "Merlin, this will be the first time you've ever seen the sky and grass and a river . . . and everything!"

The little gray foal gave a jerky hop, straight up in the air.

"Ready?" Heidi asked, appearing at the door. Behind her, Mark, Karl, and Jimmy held back, curious to see how the new foal would enjoy going out into the field. "Do you want to lead the way?"

Heidi opened the door of the stall, and they all made way for Eva and Guinevere. Little Merlin tottered close behind.

Eva led the procession across the yard and out through a side gate, down a narrow, leafy lane, and into Tom Ingleby's field. Guinevere walked steadily, stopping to snatch a mouthful of fresh green shoots growing in the hedges. Close behind her, Merlin sniffed and trotted along.

At last they reached the field. Heidi opened the gate, and Eva stepped in with Guinevere and Merlin.

The tiny foal took his first step onto lush green grass. He stayed close to his mother at first, following her every step.

Then Merlin grew braver. He moved away, taking a sniff here and a sniff there. He looked up at the vast blue sky. He tried out a small skip and a jump.

Guinevere kept a wary eye on him as he ventured out into the big, wide world.

Hey, I can jump and I can run! Merlin seemed to say. *My legs are like springs! The air smells fresh and good!*

"Look at that!" Eva murmured, sitting astride the gate as Merlin made another run and a jump. He toppled and fell to the ground, got up again, and trotted back to his mom.

"Adorable!" Heidi sighed.

Karl, Mark, and Jimmy leaned against the gate, grinning.

Eva watched Guinevere check that Merlin was okay before letting him go off to explore again. Then she glanced at the houses overlooking the field. She could see the back of the clinic, with its low roof and small windows, and next to it, the Brookses' tall white house.

"Look, he's getting braver!" Karl exclaimed as Merlin made his unsteady way up the hill, away from the river and toward the houses.

Eva saw the curtain move in a window of the Brookses' house. She caught a glimpe of Linda Brooks's face.

Yes! she thought. *Mrs. Brooks is secretly watching! I knew it. I don't care what Karl says, my plan is going to work!*

Chapter Nine

"Hey, Eva, guess what!" It was Wednesday evening and Annie came looking for her friend in the cat kennels. "I just caught Mom sneaking a peek at Merlin when she should have been doing the vacuuming!"

Eva gave a broad smile as she tucked Spice back into the basket alongside the other kittens. "Tell me more."

"Mom was upstairs vacuuming the bedrooms. I was downstairs and I heard everything go quiet. So I snuck up and found her standing at the window, just staring at Merlin in the field."

"Cool, it's working!" Eva grinned. She decided it was time to let Annie in on her plan. "Listen. My idea is to find a home for Guinevere and Merlin really nearby. I know your Aunt Ruth would take them, but I was thinking of somewhere *much* nearer than Devon."

"How much nearer?" Annie interrupted.

"So near that they wouldn't have to move at all!" Eva grinned. "My idea is to get your mom to fall in love with Merlin so she'll want to adopt him and his mom."

"When did you think of that?" Annie gasped.

"A few days ago. You gave me the idea when you said that your mom used to love ponies when she was a child."

"Yeah, I know, but . . ." Annie shrugged.

"I guess it might work. But Aunt Ruth's already said yes, and Mom's not the kind of person who backs down easily. Remember how she feels about Animal Magic."

"Come into the stables and help me muck out," Eva suggested, guiding Annie across the yard. "People change their minds," she pointed out, sticking a shovel into Annie's hands. She grinned again at the idea of Linda Brooks gazing down at the little gray foal during this, his fourth day in the sunny field. "And now that you know the plan, Annie, you have to work on your mom."

"How?"

"Tell her about Ms. Eliot never seeing Guinnie again if she goes to Devon. Remind her how wonderful ponies are, how much you'd like to have one because then you could learn to ride like she did when she was younger—all that kind of stuff."

Shovel in hand, Annie promised to try. "But don't hold your breath," she warned.

"Try!" Eva insisted, finishing the work in the stall and picking up Guinevere's bridle. "Time to bring them in from the field. Do you want to come?"

Together the girls left the yard by the side gate and went down the footpath.

Everything was calm and quiet as usual until Eva heard the sound of a car engine in the distance. "That's weird," she muttered, hurrying to the gate and spotting Guinevere and Merlin at the far side of the field.

Annie ran after her. "What is?"

"There's no way in for traffic, but I'm sure I just heard a car."

Sure enough, as she climbed the gate into Tom Ingleby's field, Eva saw a Land Rover and horse trailer crossing the old stone bridge over the river. It had driven right across the empty golf course, heading for the ponies' field.

"That's not right!" she whispered as alarm bells began to ring in her head.

Hadn't Cath Brown warned them about horse thieves in the area? And hadn't she herself seen two angry strangers supposedly fishing on the riverbank? "Oh, no!" she cried, setting off at a run. She had a vision of the two men loading Guinevere and Merlin into their trailer and driving off at top speed.

To Eva's surprise, she wasn't the first person to have spotted the Land Rover. Linda Brooks had climbed the fence in her yard and was sprinting down the field toward the bridge.

The Land Rover towed the trailer over the bridge and into the field.

"Stop!" Linda called. "This is private property. Leave the pony and her foal alone!"

Frightened by the disturbance, Guinevere and Merlin cantered off to the farthest corner of the field.

"They're horse thieves," Eva cried, beginning to panic. "We'll have to try to catch Guinevere!" She ran across the field determined to beat the thieves to it, hoping that the sight of Linda Brooks waving her arms and yelling would be enough to make them turn around.

"Mom, stop them. They're trying to steal the ponies!" Annie cried.

The Land Rover came to a halt, and two burly men stepped out.

"Turn around or I'll call the police!" Linda

insisted, going right up to the men. "You have no business being here. The golf course is private, and this field is most certainly not public property!"

The men folded their arms and stood with their feet wide apart, taking in the panicky scene.

"Hey, Guinnie, it's okay," Eva said softly as she approached the mare. At her side, little Merlin trembled and peered out from behind her. "We won't let anything bad happen." Slowly, she slipped the bridle on.

Meanwhile, Linda stood her ground. "Didn't you hear me? I said I'll call the police."

"And tell them what?" one of the men asked, the corners of his mouth twitching as he tried not to smile. "That Tom Ingleby sent us to set up some electric fencing?"

Linda stared. "Tom Ingleby?" she echoed.

The man nodded. "He's our boss. The fence posts are in the trailer if you'd like to check it out."

"Fence posts?" Taking a deep breath, Linda walked around the back of the trailer and looked inside. "Hmm," she muttered. "I thought . . . I mean . . . I was watching from my window. I thought you were trespassing. And the girls here—they said you were horse thieves!"

"You can't be too careful," the man agreed. "I'm Dan Shaw. And this is Nathan. Nathan, get the boss on your cell phone and get him to tell Mrs...."

"—Brooks," Linda mumbled. She was red and hot, her blonde hair stuck to her forehead.

"Get him to tell Mrs. Brooks that we are who we say we are."

"That won't be necessary," Linda

stammered, calling to Annie and Eva that everything was okay. "I'm awfully sorry, Mr. Shaw. You must think I'm a total idiot!"

Slowly, Eva led Guinevere and Merlin toward the men with the trailer. Merlin trotted calmly beside Annie.

Dan Shaw grinned. "I pity any poor horse thief who tries to steal those two. With you three around, they wouldn't stand a chance!"

Linda's blushes deepened. "Annie, Eva, meet Dan and Nathan. They work for Tom Ingleby."

Eva gulped. Annie groaned. But the two men chuckled and said they would come back to do the fencing some other time, when the field was empty. Then they climbed into the Land Rover and drove away slowly.

"Oh, wow!" Eva muttered, and shook her head.

At his mother's side, Merlin suddenly took a little skip and hop toward Linda.

"Ah!" Annie sighed.

As Eva looked on quietly, she noticed Karl dashing across the field toward them.

"What happened?" he called. "How come Tom's men drove off without doing their job?"

Eva, Annie, and Linda stared at him.

"You knew about Dan and Nathan?" Eva asked.

Karl nodded. "I answered a phone call from Tom Ingleby earlier this afternoon. He said to expect his men to turn up to set up some electric fencing."

"Thanks for telling us!" Eva groaned.

"Uh-oh. Why do I get the feeling that my little sis just jumped to the wrong conclusion, as usual?" Karl laughed.

"I'm afraid we all did," Linda confessed. She stroked Merlin and smiled as he hopped a little closer. Then he stuck out his nose and nuzzled her hand.

"Oh, how dreadful it would have been if those men really had been horse thieves!" Linda sighed. Gently, she stroked the foal's soft nose. She went down on her knees and rested her cheek against his neck. "You're beautiful!" she whispered. "I'm sorry if we scared you, but I thought those men were coming to steal you, and I couldn't let that happen!"

Annie nodded at Eva, who smiled back.

"You're totally adorable!" Linda murmured. She looked up at Eva with a tearful face. "What's his name?"

"Merlin," Eva replied.

"Like the wizard," Linda whispered. "Well, Merlin, you've worked your magic on me!"

Chapter Ten

"So, you see, we think it would be a wonderful idea if Guinevere and Merlin could stay in Okeham," Linda Brooks told Heidi and Mark.

She'd stopped by the house with Annie late on Wednesday evening just as Jimmy Harrison had arrived with Ms. Eliot to pick up Tigger.

The farmhouse kitchen was full of visitors, all drinking tea around the big pine table. Annie sat beside Eva and Karl with an enormous grin on her face.

Mark cleared his throat. "Let me get this straight, Linda. Are you actually offering a home to the pony and her foal?"

Linda nodded. "I've talked with my sister, Ruth, on the phone, and she agrees it's by far the best solution to keep them here. I've also spoken to Tom Ingleby, who's perfectly happy to keep on renting us the field at the back of our house. And of course, Jason agrees that it will be good for Annie to have a pony."

"Whoa!" Mark muttered, holding up both hands. "Did I miss something?" he whispered to Eva.

The shock waves of Linda's offer allowed Ms. Eliot to break into the conversation. "Oh, it would be wonderful to be able to visit Guinevere!" she sighed. "It softens the blow of having to sell Ash Tree Manor if I know I can still see my beautiful pony!"

"And her new foal!" Eva added. She had a warm glow in her stomach, knowing that Animal Magic had once more done its work to match the perfect pet with the perfect owner.

"Well, Annie, there's no need to ask how you feel about the arrangement!" Heidi smiled. "I can tell by the look on your face that you think you're in heaven."

"Pinch me, someone!" Annie sighed. "I'm actually going to have my own pony. Eva, because this is all thanks to you, you can ride Guinevere whenever you want!"

"Now someone has to pinch *me* and make me believe what's happening!" Eva exclaimed, closing her eyes and picturing herself riding Guinnie by the river, with Merlin trotting along at their side.

Heidi turned back to Linda. "And does this mean you'll be withdrawing your petition to have us closed down?"

An embarrassed frown appeared on Linda's face. "I'm afraid it's too late for that. Mr. Winters tells me that he's in the middle of writing his report."

"So we'll have to wait and see." Mark nodded.

"Oh, dear, oh, dear," Ms. Eliot said softly. "I had no idea!"

"Come and see Merlin?" Eva cut in, eager to change the subject. She, Annie, and Karl led the old woman out to the stables. The grown-ups followed behind.

There, in the glow of the lamp, Guinevere stood guard over her foal. She raised her head and whinnied as Ms. Eliot approached.

"Who's my clever girl!" The old lady sighed, gazing down at Merlin. "What a beautiful little creature you are!"

Merlin looked up from his bed of straw. He was too sleepy to get up, though he raised his head and flicked his ears toward the visitors.

"Wonderful!" Ms. Eliot murmured, with tears in her eyes.

Karl stood with his hands in his pockets, doing the don't-show-your-emotions boy thing. But Eva felt her own tears well up. Guinevere and Merlin would never be more than a stone's throw from Animal Magic. It was a dream come true.

Annie couldn't help it. She cried in full view of everyone. "I'm just so-o-o happy!" she sniffed.

And Merlin settled down in his warm bed and slept.

Look out for the next book in the series!

Rusty

The injured fox cub

Everyone enjoys having Rusty the fox cub
stay at Animal Magic, especially Eva, who
can't help treating him as a pet.
Eva knows that the cub must be returned
to the wild, but has her loving
care ruined Rusty's chances of
being set free?